Little Granny Quarterback

by Bill Martin Jr and Michael Sampson

Illustrated by Michael Chesworth

Boyds Mills Press

Published by Caroline House
Boyds Mills Press, Inc.
A Highlights Company
815 Church Street
Honesdale, Pennsylvania 18431
Printed in China

U.S. Cataloging-in-Publication Data
    (Library of Congress Standards)

Martin, Bill.
    Little granny quarterback / by Bill Martin Jr and Michael Sampson ;
illustrated by Michael Chesworth. — 1st ed.
[32] p. : col. ill. ;   cm.
Summary: Granny envisions what it would be like to be a star quarterback
football player as she was when she was young.
ISBN 1-56397-930-6
1. Grandmothers. 2. Quarterback (Football) — Fiction. I. Sampson, Michael.
II. Chesworth, Michael, ill. III. Title.
  [E]   21   2001   CIP   AC
00-112041

First edition, 2001
The text of this book is set in 16-point School Bus Bounce Normal.

10 9 8 7 6 5 4 3 2 1

To Ida Sampson—my friend and fellow football fan
—BMJ

To my brother Bill
—MS

Little Granny Whiteoak,
reading in bed,
perked her ears
when the TV said,

"Ball's on the forty,
still enough time.
We need Granny!
The game's on the line!"

"Presto, change-o!
Gridiron gold!
Up and at 'em, Granny.
Go! Go! Go!"

Granny looks at the wall
where her trophies are hung.
She remembers back,
when she was young.

Clippings tell of a great career,
except two headlines
that bring back a tear:

WHITEOAK FUMBLES;
LOSES GAME!

NO CHANCE FOR PLAYOFFS NOW

SO CLOSE

QB QUITS,
NO MORE FAME

GO GRANNY

OWL
S
K

Granny takes a deep breath,
wriggles her toes.
Aches and pains say,
"No! No! No!"

Should she quit?
Give up her dream?
Is she too old
for the football team?

Up! Up! Up!
She jumps out of bed.
Flippity flop!
She stands on her head.

She clicks her heels,
grabs her cane,
and off she trots
to the football game.

Little Granny Quarterback
runs on the field,
joins the huddle,
and the fans all cheer!

"24! 36! Hut! Hut! Hut!"

Snap from the center—
What will she do?

She leaps!

She jumps!

She twists!

She runs!

She hits the line.
The ball squirts free.

Stumble!

Fumble!

Whose ball will it be?

Little Granny Quarterback scoops up the ball!
She lifts her helmet and sticks out her jaw.

Clap!
Crunch!
Churn!
Turn!

She weaves to the left,
dances to the right,
and drives for redemption
with all her might.

Bulldog Durham
stands in the way.
"Flatten him, Granny,
make it your day!"

She's so small,
he's so tall,
but the bigger they are,
the harder they fall.

Granny sees stars.
Can she still go?

Little Granny Quarterback
soars through the sky . . .

hits the end zone.
The fans all cry . . .

"Touchdown, touchdown, Sis! Boom! Bah!"

**"Little Granny Quarterback,
Rah!
Rah!
Rah!"**

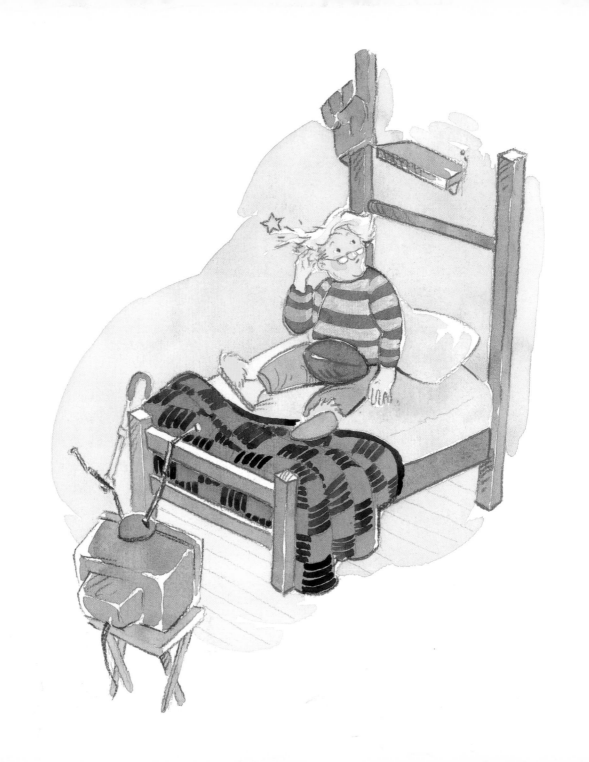